The Adventures of
SPARROWBOY

The Adventures of SPARR

SCHOLASTIC INC.
New York Toronto London Auckland
Sydney New Delhi Hong Kong

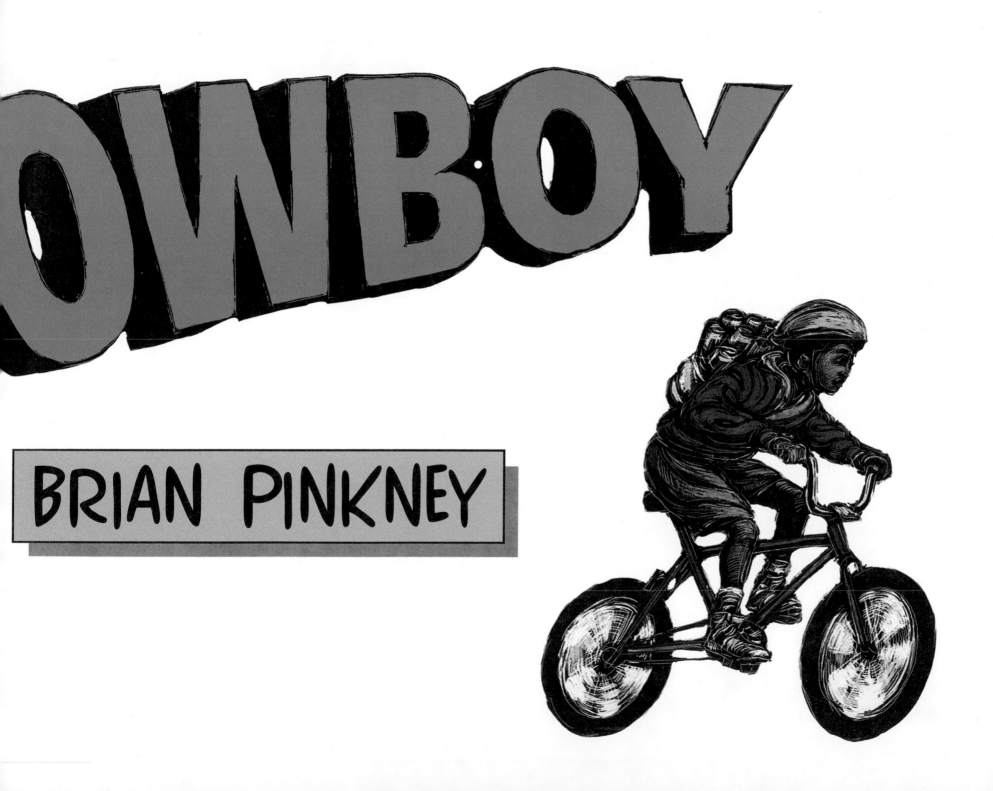

OWBOY

BRIAN PINKNEY

Copyright © 1997 by Brian Pinkney.
All rights reserved.
Published by Scholastic Inc., 557 Broadway, New York, NY 10012,
by arrangement with Aladdin Paperbacks,
an imprint of Simon & Schuster Children's Publishing Division.
Printed in the U.S.A.

ISBN-13: 978-0-545-87258-4
ISBN-10: 0-545-87258-8

6 7 8 9 10   40   24 23 22 21 20 19 18 17 16

Henry the paperboy always read the front page before he started on his route. Then he read the comics.

Sometimes, the headlines got Henry down. "Why does this stuff have to happen?" he asked himself. "If Falconman was here, he'd make things better."

The Adventures of
BY BARNEY NIPKIN

FALCON

THERE'S REAL TROUBLE BELOW!

It's a job for Falconman!

HELP!

MAN

It has come to pass that a mystical falcon possesses the gift to transfer his powers to a mortal. That man is Trooper Mark Steed who becomes . . . Falconman, a superhero sworn to defend the defenseless.

ZAP!

WHOOSH!

"Going my way?"

Man and bird return to the transfer site.

ZAP!

To be continued...

Later, as Henry rode along Thurber Street tossing papers onto porches, a sparrow swooped down and landed in the middle of his path.

"Hey! Get out of my way!" Henry jammed on the brakes and . . .

Henry flew over the handlebars and soared to the sky.

"You were almost a sparrow sandwich," Henry said.

MEANWHILE . . . BRUNO WAS STILL UP TO NO GOOD.

"Hey, Dawn! Does your cat have nine lives?"

"Hey, Bruno! Do you???"

THONK!

"... Have a nice ride!"

"Now you see him, now you don't!" said Henry.

"You'll be out of danger there," Henry said, "and I can finish delivering my papers."

"I don't get it. Why can't you fly?"

THERE'S JUST ONE WAY TO FIND OUT!

Together, Henry and the sparrow returned

to the place where they had first collided.

All was quiet along Thurber
Street as Henry rode home. Trouble
was nowhere to be seen.

And everything felt just a little better.